Unspoken words from a LOUD MOUTH

Eric Harris

Contents

Acknowledgment

A special thanks to the following people

Tierny Lesueur

Samuel Merino

Nyah Smith

Gianna Correa

Alex Danzy

Jolie Ross

Even though I wrote every single poem in this book. I couldn't do it without y'all. From late night phone calls or almost giving up my book. I thank you for always encouraging me and always pushing me to do better

I also want to give a big shoutout to my family & my congregation.

And I definitely cannot forget to give my thanks and all my love to my amazing coworkers & managers at Starbucks & P.F Changs

None of this would be possible without you guys.

Instagram: @itsjust_ericc
Email: ericharris977@yahoo.com

Introduction

I decided to write a whole book just about poems.
not really a poet but it better than writing songs
These poems will be about my past. the present and most of all to the future
of course, just talking about these things will bring me pain
but an imperfect mind means an imperfect brain
so instead of getting on a plane and disappear from my problems
I'd rather let the strong winds and the heavy rain come and wash all of my problems
away.

From The Past

Death overtakes us all

people ain't even close to a being a millionaire
but yet they so concerned about being the next billionaire
so they work all the time
saving all their little dimes
so they can buy the big house on the hill
but they forgot stress kills
but they do anything to reach that milestone
they sacrifice so much that they end up alone
so when they end up dead and gone
nobody is visiting their tombstone
all because they wanted to be the next bill gate
but couldn't see there nothing behind that gate
except hate and i guess it too late to tell them
It was the graveyard diggers who were making the most bank.

Seasonal Depression

the trees are changing colors
the weather is getting chilly
autumn is here and the only thing i was falling for is you
everything about you were like a cozy blanket on a cold night
people texting me but the only one i was waiting for was from you
or should i say that how it was in the beginning?
because it the middle of october and everyone looking for costumes
but you were already in one because how do you claim to be so godly but you
with ghouls and goblins at night? when the information was brought to light
It sounded like lightning and thunder. My thoughts became *gloomy*.
that bright burning bush that used to be my heart was withering aways
I guess those sweet things you told me were just candy laced with poison?
All those things you told me made me sick. Even my grandmother's chicken
noodle soup couldn't make me feel better but instead of questioning you, I
question myself.

I gave you the whole art museum but you are outside looking at the trash
Is that what you call art?
Is that what you like?
or am i worth less than that?

I can't believe I became insecure about something that wasn't so secure.

I can't believe I wasted all my time on you
I can't believe I almost gave up my life for you.
I can't believe I almost gave up my relationship with my God for you.

The color of my mind

Sometimes it felt like I was in an illusion because of all the colors
that was in my mind it was so confusing to tell what was real and what wasn't.

So as an artist, I try to paint things so they can see what going on with me
I painted my room gray just like the cloud that was above my head that I
could only see.

All the raindrops coming from my eyes could grow a sequoia tree but instead,
it just felt like it was drowning me.

So I decided to write poems to help me express myself but all they had to say
was "Wow that deep".

Yes my sorrows are deep and blue like the Atlantic sea
Floating with the garbage where it ain't supposed to be
Now my personality became like my favorite colors
My eyes became green and I was full with envy
My body became red and I was furious
And my thoughts became black like a dark night & there was no light to save
me.

Slowing Growing

I still think about how people used to treat me at a young age
They made me feel like I was an animal in a cage
Then got mad at me because I was fueled with rage
So I write these poems to help me cope
But sometimes I feel like there is no hope
Because I keep hearing people talk about me behind the stage and I want to
go on a rampage
But I won't even engage because I've been working on myself so much lately.
I won't even bring that bad energy on stage so instead of me talking about it.

Let's just move on to the next page

November 10th, 2018

How can I be connected to the earth when I'm not connected to the creator?
How can I know the names of certain stars but not the name of the most
high?

So let me give credit, my life, and all the glory to God
The creator of all things such as the Nova
Name known as Jehovah
I thank you for making my life bright
Even when life gets dark you remind me you are still there
By painting the night sky with the northern lights
I thank you for giving me wisdom just like Solomon
But just like father like son sometimes I let my desire get the best of me
But I will continue writing you psalms just like David

I thank you for changing my life around just like Saul
Now I get to declare the good news just like Paul
I thank you for not looking down on my youth
I thank you for allowing my grandmother to teach
me the precious truths and giving me the Bible that provides faithful ones in
history just like Timothy
This world is full of toxicity & I thank you for breaking me free from captivity

Even though people make fun of me because of my dedication.
But I don't care because serving you feels like a vacation. I will keep building
up my faith so I can have a strong foundation. I will try my best to pass every
temptation. I might learn a different language to help with the translation.

Just like the prophet Isaiah, "Here I am, send me" to any location so I can
help people earn salvation because I'm only a slave to the most high but it
never feels like a plantation.

The Present

New Beginnings

Even though i'm no longer in the past
I would say i'm happy at last but I still have bad days
But i'm happy that i'm taking my life more serious
No longer viewing my life as a game of dice
Had to remove these negative thoughts from my head like lice
The sun is out so my heart is no longer full of ice
But once my life got sunny people started saying i was acting funny

Even though people are still cold like the weather
I still try my best to be gentle like a feather
I can't let these thieves rob me of my joy
Can't even let them get a piece because
They will think they have a lease

People might think i'm quiet because I keep it brief
But to be completely honest i'm so concerned about my peace

Botanical Garden

They say every flower have a purpose
if that is the case then why do people who claim to be gentle and beneficial
like aloe vera is toxic? Mr. Dandelion always bragging about how he got
a ph.d. or how much he had an impact on my life. I don't have a strong
memory like an elephant but when's the last time you helped me? The last
time I check
you were just another weed in my garden that wasn't helping my growth
now they are reading my poems saying 'dude why you gotta be rude?"
rude? Imagine roses bragging about their petals but don't have any?
But I guess I have to forgive and forget. This exactly why I hang out with
Mr and Mrs Lavender who helped me put my past to rest and helped me to
repel the pests who just want drama. I definitely can't forget the children of
the sunflowers field who brighten my day and help me follow the light.
Jehovah God knew I was sick of life so he blessed me with people who had
that vitamin c.

Now the weeds of my past ask why I'm so obsessed with plants.
I'm not obsessed. I just don't stress myself with people anymore.
I just hung out with many people who made me second guess myself
when I was depressed. Nobody addresses it. Instead, they were so pressed
about some mess. So instead of hanging out with people who made me upset
I just left and progress

man, I should just change my name to Erykah Badu because "didn't cha
know" I pick my friends like I pick my fruits so I won't be like Eve picking
fruits from the forbidden tree.

Unsent love letter

Something about you got me thinking I can find love again
Spring is here so doves are flying in the air and you might be my perfect pair
But as the magnolia trees start to bloom it reminds me I'm not past the bloom of youth
So am I thinking right? But every time I'm around you everything feels right
But am I ready to fall in love again? Just because I'm over my ex doesn't mean I should move on to the next. They always tell me there are plenty of fish in the sea
But I don't want them, I wanted you. I don't believe in fairy tales but you can be my Princess Ariel but how can I tell you I want to be part of your world if Ursula not only stole my voice but my courage to talk to you? Now you're gone and this is just another poem I'm writing about how I'm alone.

I guess some things never change

Minds Games

Social media is another word for mind games
Because when you look in the mirror you a Naomi
But social media don't care for true beauty so they portray you as lonely
Now you see all these people boldly sharing their beauty secret
But they are getting their looks off Adobe.
This world is full of false paintings that will try to change your mind
But don't let them cultivate your mind because you are a Mona Lisa in disguise
Even though you might be lost and confused Like Alice
And Your mind might be disturbed like Van Gogh
But in reality, you are a starry night that will brighten up anyone night

Truth be told you just Lost
Art that hasn't been discovered yet because if
The art museum found you they will
Indicate your beauty
And your amazing personality but instead
You just stay hidden from this
Negative world that will try to make you depressed

Please Don't get stressed
Because you are the best at everything you put your mind to.

You might not feel like it right now but you are truly blessed.

Dear little brown boys

Dear little brown boys, I hope you know you are a force of nature
How your hair defy gravity got you floating in the sky
Even when you cut it short. The moon will create waves in your hair
just like the waves of the seas
I know the media will make you swim in a certain direction but
please realize you don't belong in those streets.
Please realize your beautiful brown skin is rich and nourishing just
like soil meaning you can grow into anything you want to be.
Your sadness and your tears is not a sign of weakness because you
still strong like a redwood tree

To The Future

At Last

Even though we are watching our loved ones wither away like flowers in the
winter times.
We have to remember spring is around the corner and they will blossom and
just like Maya Angelou they will rise.
The homeless will no longer grieve or sigh because they will have a house at a
nice size.
No more pollution just bright blue skies
No more living in a world full of lies just guided by the most high and wise
Even though it sounds like a fairy tale. Jehovah will definitely give us this prize
No longer will have to write my thirteen reason why
Because I will no longer be troubled by my past
Because there will be peace on earth at last.

Dear Ma

Even though you weren't there when I learn how to walk
even though you weren't there to see your baby boy with his cap & gown.
just know it wasn't your fault, life had other plans for you.

I hear so many stories about the risk you took in life.
i'm writing a book about poems but I can write a whole novel about you
but yet they still will say i'm not talking about you enough
maybe I should change my name to Abba just to say mama mia, does it show
again how much i've missed you? Just to explain, my skin is brown but I have
been blue since the day you parted.But I can't focus on that. Just know I've
been thinking about you since Nia Long played on the first friday.

 dang, wait has it been that long? Even though I have a forgetful memory.
One thing I'll never forgot is you, just know I'm listening to Tamia while
writing this because I'm officially missing you

I will never stop thinking about you. I know you are resting in peace but soon
you will be resurrected in paradise and I can't wait for that. So once again
don't get upset you weren't there to take me to my first prom. You will be
there to walk me down the aisle to see your baby boy getting married.

Say Yes

I'm not the type of person you always see on the basketball court
Because I'm always at home and since I'm always alone
I'm just gonna write a poem about it...While I'm listening
To the gentle Rain that taps against my window & the Buzzing
noise that comes from bees, forgot to mention my favorite music is R&B

So can we just lie down in the sunflower field and talk about life while we
listen to some blues,
Because I feel just like Brandy because all I'm doing is Sittin' Up In My Room
writing poems and I almost wrote a poem about the moon but instead I'm
writing about you,
Can't you take a clue that I'm into you?
Maybe later we can watch sum Blue Clues so he can help you figure it out but
if you not feeling what I'm Feeling just tell me the truth
But if you are then let's continue this journey so when we are watching
Sherlock Holmes...
Our kids don't even have to investigate why their mom and dad got married

The best come last

Even though you was the first one who won the race
I didn't see you when I came in second place
How did you disappear that quickly?
I also didn't see you when I needed you the most
you also wasn't there to teach me the simple things
such as 1 2 3 I always had my numbers backwards
so don't get confused when I tell you
Eric the third will alway come first in my life
even though I didn't understand everything
I'm not mad at you. Because every time
I look in the mirror I see you
I forgave and let go
I grew from the mistakes
And I just learn how to do better.

Tag, You're It

This book might feel short
But it took forever for me to write it
From sleepless night to procrastination
I thought I will never get done with this book

But I did.

It was so hard trying to unlock memories. I tossed away There were some
nights I got sad just thinking of my past
There were some nights I laughed
There were some nights I wanted to give up

But I didn't.

I wish I could tell you how much work went into this book but I just mentally
& emotionally can't but I thank you for going through this emotional
rollercoaster with me and purchasing and reading my book.

We might not be on a playground but Tag, You're it.
It's your turn to start writing & I can't wait to read what you put out.

About the author.

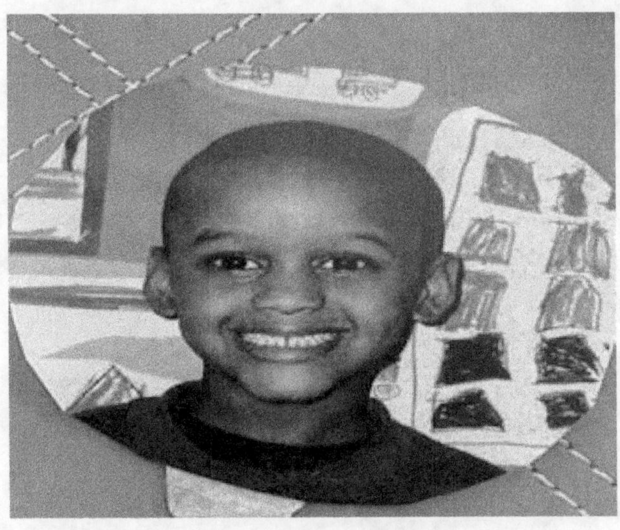

My name is Eric Harris. I was born and raised in Milwaukee Wisconsin. As a young boy, I was often bullied for my height, my voice, and my size. So I was very insecure and I didn't think people understood me so I decided to write poems. The art of poetry came from my father. He has an amazing ability to come up with rhyme as he writes raps about his life. It impressed me but instead of rapping, I decided to write poems about my life. So I decided to write a whole book dedicated to poems.

While I love to write poems. I also love using my free time to teach people about the Bible. I love to travel the world and I almost forgot to give thanks to the three little boys I met in Guatemala who helped me to be more grateful and humble in life. I also love being involved in nature which actually gave me more inspiration and ideas to write these poems. I'm not the best but I also dabble in graphic design and I actually design my own book cover.(quick shout-out to Ms. Nettesheim for teaching me that amazing skill) that's enough about me but if you would like to learn more about the things I do. My Instagram is on page 3.